# Waddling Walter Runs Away to the Wide, Wide World

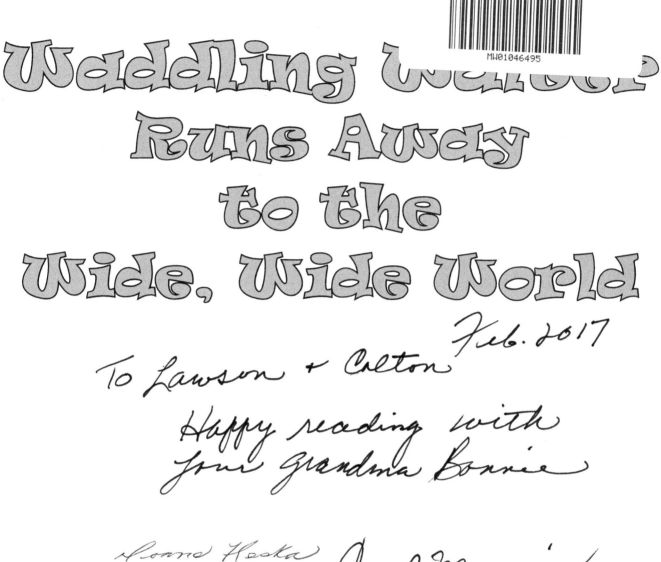

*To Lawson + Colton* Feb. 2017

*Happy reading with your Grandma Bonnie*

Donna Flaska and Carol Margosein

PAGE PUBLISHING, INC.
New York, NY

First originally published by Page Publishing, Inc. 2017

ISBN 978-1-68409-035-8 (Paperback)
ISBN 978-1-68409-037-2 (Hard Cover)
ISBN 978-1-68409-036-5 (Digital)

Printed in the United States of America

Dedicated to Libby

A Wise Old Soul

One glorious spring morning, after all the animals in the barnyard were fed, a truck pulled into the driveway.

The man yelled from the truck, "Anyone home?"

Kelly, owner and friend to all the animals in the barnyard, came to the door.

She asked, "Can I help you?"

He replied, "I would like to buy that large black-and-white goat. I will pay you a lot of money for that goat."

The man was talking about Walter. Walter was a mean goat, who only got along with Libby, the llama. He liked to wander the farm and be the tough guy. At hearing what the man said, Walter raised his head.

Walter thought, *There are many reasons Kelly would get rid of me. I do not like the other animals because they get in my way. I eat a lot. I can be mean to everyone, including humans.*

Walter thought about the other day, when he cornered a man who petted him the wrong way. He pushed him up against the barn wall.

Kelly looked at Walter, then looked at the man in the truck.

She said, "Let me talk to you privately."

Walter was so hurt that Kelly would even talk to the man that he stormed off to his barn.

Walter thought, *How dare she think of getting rid of me?*

Walter did not know that Kelly told the man, "Thanks for the offer, but Walter is not for sale."

Libby heard everything that was said and knew that Walter would take it all wrong.

"I must escape and run off before she sells me," Walter thought out loud. "No one must know where I am going so Kelly cannot find me. It is time for me to leave the barnyard anyway."

8

Kelly loved the younger goats because they were so playful. One of those goats was Puey, a little clown and stinker. Puey and his friend, Lolly, liked to play on the slide. Kelly loved Libby because she was a great, old soul.

Kelly loved the donkey, Orlando, because he played with her. Orlando, wiggling and giggling, backed up to his bristle brush, waiting for Kelly to play.

12

Kelly loved Willie because he was an intelligent pig. Willie had a house, a pool, a sandbox, and lots of toys. Walter wished that he had toys, but everyone knew that he broke them.

Walter thought out loud, "Where does that leave me?" He thought, *Kelly does not love me anymore, so I will go out into the wide, wide world and find someone to love me.*

After dark, Walter pushed all his weight against the fence so he could roll over it and be out of his pen. He was free! Free to travel the wide, wide world. No more pesky Puey playing tricks on him. No more spoiled Willie Banks and all his toys. Finally, no more Orlando's *he-haw*ing. At last, Walter was on his way.

Libby saw Walter run away and wondered how to tell Kelly.

As Walter walked down the long driveway, he got very tired. Walter was tired because he was heavy and should be asleep, not knocking down fences and running down the driveway. He was so tired that he decided to take a quick nap under the mailbox.

He thought, *There is plenty of time to start my new adventure,* and he fell instantly asleep.

As the sun peeked out of the clouds, the newspaperboy tossed the paper. He hit Walter on the head and woke him up. Walter thought, *it was so early that Red (the rooster) and Martha (the hen) are not even up.*

Walter said to himself, "I have to get out of here before Kelly wakes up. Time to see the world and find someone to love me." Walter said it over and over.

He walked into the woods so no one could see him. A little red fox peeked at him; the hawks flew overhead, and the owls hooted at each other. Walter walked for a long time deep into the dark, quiet woods. Soon, Walter could see a full moon. Bats kept flying around his head, and he became scared. He shook with fear as he wondered which way to go. A hoot owl came by and landed in a tree. Walter walked over to the tree and saw that moss was growing on the north side of the tree.

Walter thought, *I will go north.*

As he walked, the hoot owl flew next to him. Walter liked the owl because he thought the owl was helping him, and he was.

After a while, lightning and thunder appeared right over Walter's head. He got scared again. The hoot owl led him to a pile of rocks, so Walter hid inside the pile and fell asleep.

Morning came more beautiful than ever, and Walter woke up very hungry. He wiggled out from under the rocks and began to wish that he was back on Kelly's farm. He walked and walked and came upon a stream, swollen from the rain. He couldn't cross it, so he sat down on the bank of the stream. Walter was cold, hungry, tired, and lonely. He missed Libby, and he even missed Puey. Walter cried him-self to sleep as he lay on the ground. His friend, the owl, kept watch in the night.

It was not quite dawn, and Walter heard cock-a-doodle-do!

Walter said to the owl, "Is that Red, the rooster?"

He looked around and saw a familiar path—a path he had taken a walk on with Kelly. He got all embarrassed because he traveled in a circle.

He thought, *I am home, I am back and can see Kelly and all the other animals.*

Walter kept thinking about the food he would eat once he got home, so he walked quickly up the path.

29

Walter walked into the barnyard, and all the other animals let out a big shout.

Kelly thought, *Now what?*

She was worried and tired from looking for Walter. She ran outside and saw him. She ran up to Walter and gave him a big hug.

She said to him, "Walter, no matter what you do, this is where you belong. This is your home, and we love you. This also goes for all the rest of you."

All the animals in the barnyard cheered because Walter was home.

Walter thought, *I will never do this again. Besides, the food is too good.*

# About the Authors

Donna Flaska is a grandmother of fifteen grandchildren and two great-grandchildren. She believes the story about Walter will be enjoyed by them. She is a former business owner, now retired and enjoying creative endeavors.

Carol Margosein is a grandmother of one school-age girl. She is a retired teacher after thirty-five years. She taught elementary, junior high, high school, and college. She holds a PhD in Literacy and Culture.

CPSIA information can be obtained
at www.ICGtesting.com
Printed in the USA
LVOW06s0428010217

522787LV00003B/4/P

9 781684 090358